What's That Noise?

by Mary Roennfeldt

illustrated by Robert Roennfeldt

Orchard Books
New York

It was very late, very dark, and very quiet...

when George heard a funny noise. He closed his book and listened carefully.

He put on his coat and slippers
and tiptoed across the floor,
listening all the time.

He couldn't
imagine what
would make
such a funny
noise.

George shone
his flashlight on
the green leaves,

he walked to the
end of the path,

and he opened
the gate.

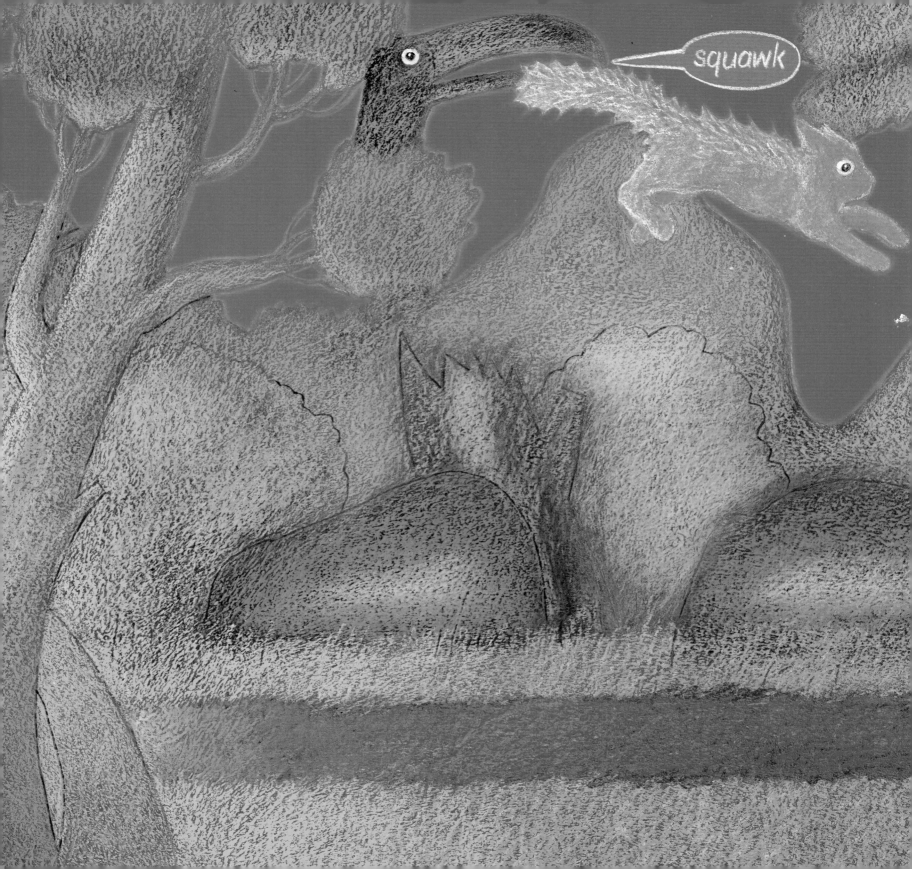

He looked...

and looked...

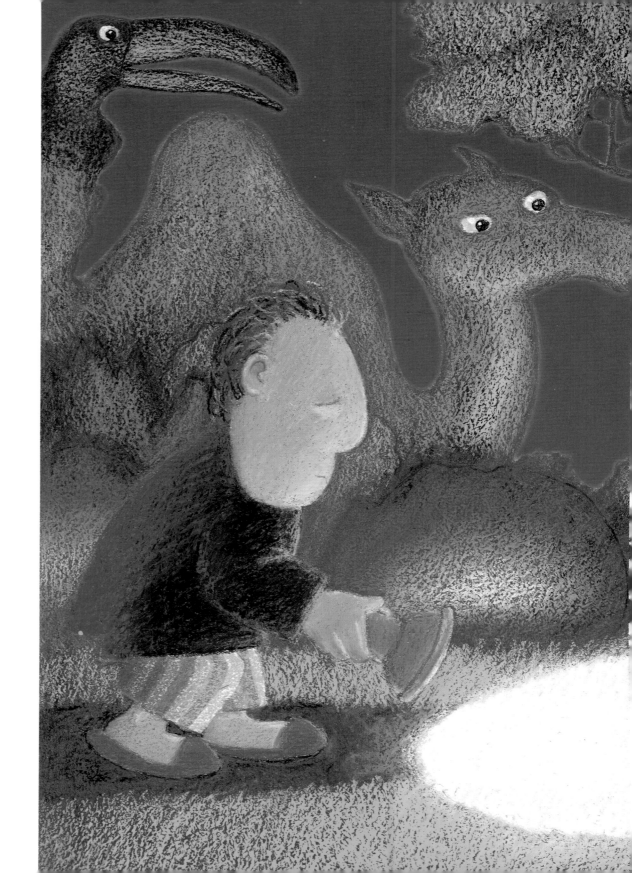

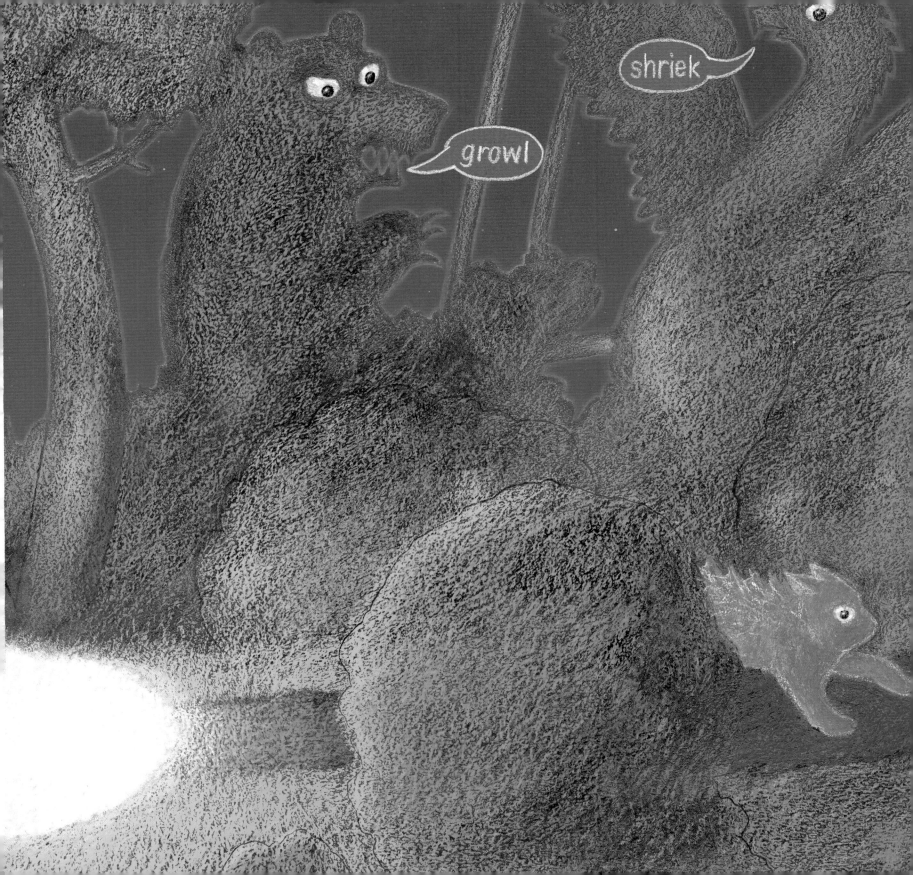

and looked...

but he could not
see anything
that would
make such a
funny noise.

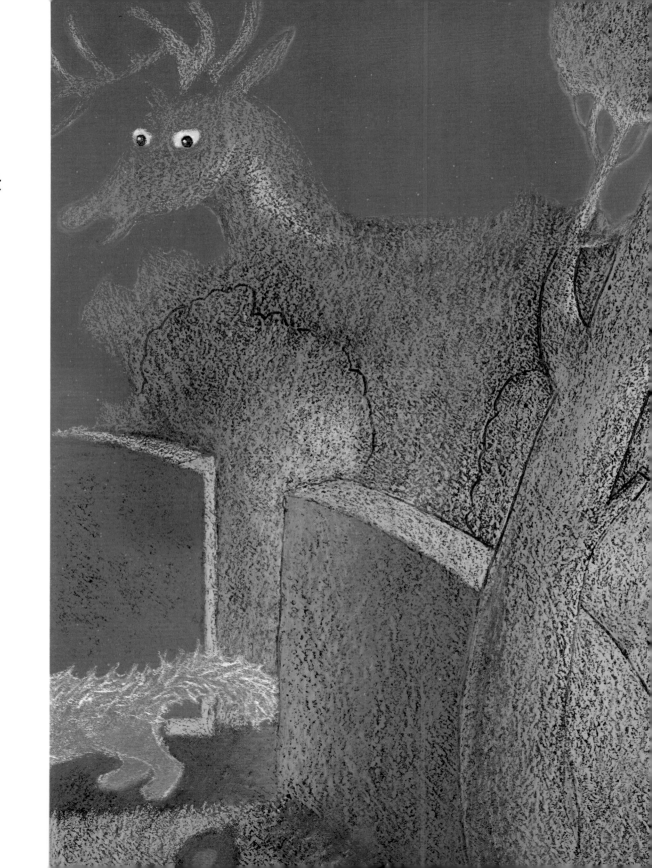

He turned off the flashlight and
went back to bed.

In the morning George was very tired.
He could barely keep his eyes open.

All day long, George wondered what had made the funny noise in the night.

The rest of the zoo knew.
Do you?

For Lyn

Orchard Books
387 Park Avenue South
New York, NY 10016

Manufactured in the United States of America
Printed by Barton Press, Inc.
Bound by Horowitz/Rae
Book design by Susan Phillips
The text of this book is set in 20 point Palatino Bold.

10 9 8 7 6 5 4 3 2 1

Library of Congress Cataloging-in-Publication Data
Roennfeldt, Mary.
  What's that noise? / by Mary Roennfeldt ; illustrated by Robert Roennfeldt.
    p.   cm.
  Summary: A zookeeper hears a strange noise at night and searches in vain for
its origin.
  ISBN 0-531-05972-3   ISBN 0-531-08572-4 (lib. bdg.)   [1. Zoos—Fiction.
2. Sound—Fiction.   3. Cats—Fiction.]   I. Roennfeldt, Robert, ill.   II. Title.
PZ7.R6254Wh   1992   [E]—dc20   91-16215